A Family Magic

Cursed
Dishes

"This spell is starting to bug me."

by Jennifer Lott
illustrated by Doriano Strologo

Cursed Dishes
Book 1 of the Family Magic Series

Copyright © 2014 by Jennifer Lott

Reality Skimming Press
An Imprint of Okal Rel Universe
201-9329 University Crescent, Burnaby, BC, V5A 4Y4, Canada

Interior design: Lynda Williams
Cover & interior art: Doriano Strologo
ISBN: 978-0-9921402-3-6

Library and Archives Canada Cataloguing in Publication

Lott, Jennifer, 1987-., author
      Cursed dishes / Jennifer Lott, author; Doriano Strologo, Illustrator.

(Family magic ; 1)
ISBN 978-0-9921402-3-6 (pbk.)

      I. Strologo, Doriano, 1964-, illustrator II. Title.

PS8623.O87C87 2014   JC813'.6   C2014-900842-2

First Edition
(C-20140418)

Dedication

For my prepublication fans,
especially the children.

To Oliver

Enjoy :)

jenlott

Visit the author's website at jenniferlott.com

Chapter 1

Charlotte and Eileen went to elementary school and were only two years apart. For them, homework was rare and chores optional. So they led their young lives happy and free.

Life might have always been a thing of beauty had it not been for their older sister Glenda.

Glenda was sixteen, had homework every day, did her own laundry and washed the dishes twice a week.

Charlotte and Eileen wouldn't have minded except that Glenda was always trying to drag them into the world of hard work too. She would often ask that they "clean up after themselves" or "deal with natural consequences" as if they were grownups!

"Charlotte!" said Glenda, one Thursday afternoon while she was washing dishes.

"You didn't scrape out your leftover cereal this morning. It's disgusting. Come and scrape it out now."

"I can't," called Charlotte from the computer in the next room. "I'm too busy blowing things up. If I don't blow up ten things in the next five seconds, I'll die!"

Glenda waited five seconds. "Can you come and do it now?" she asked.

"No!" yelled Charlotte. "I'm on the next level now and there are hundreds of new things to blow up. I don't have time for cereal bowls; that's your job."

"My job is to wash dirty *dishes*, not soggy *cereal*. It's your mess and I am sick of cleaning up after you. So unless you're planning to finish eating it, you need to—"

"I'm not listening," sang

Charlotte.

Glenda slammed the bowl down on the counter in fury.

Charlotte braced herself for more yelling. When Glenda next spoke, however, it was in a strangely calm voice.

"Are you sure you won't scrape out your leftover cereal?" she asked.
Charlotte was sure. "Yes," she said.

Glenda brought the bowl back to the rest of the dishes, held it before her and whispered: "Schiebe die Schuld wo sie gehört!" She then continued her work as though nothing had happened.

Charlotte went on playing her computer game. She wondered why Glenda had dropped the subject of dishes so calmly, but she was far too busy blowing things up to worry much about it.

Chapter 2

In the early hours of the morning, Charlotte was sleeping peacefully. She was dreaming a happy dream about school closing early and her birthday happening every day of the year.

Her alarm clock rang at 7:30 a.m. Charlotte turned it off without opening her eyes.

Then she noticed a strange smell. There was a weird feeling about her left foot. Sitting up in bed, she looked down and screamed. Her heel was stuck in a bowl of soggy cereal.

"Oh!" cried Charlotte. "Oh, oh, guh-ross!"

She fell out of bed, knocking the bowl to the floor. Ignoring the spilled cereal, she ran for the bathroom and scrubbed her foot clean.

"How? Why? How?" she asked herself confusedly, as she went back to her room and covered the spilled cereal with a rug.

Then it dawned on her: Glenda! Glenda must've got so tired of doing her dishes that she had decided to shove the nastiest ones off on innocent people.

"But," said Charlotte to herself, "she's not going to get away with it."

Grinning wickedly, Charlotte went to Glenda's bedroom. It was empty because Glenda had left for band practice at 7:15 a.m. She pulled back the covers of Glenda's bed and placed the bowl upside-down beneath them.

She ground the remaining dregs of cereal into Glenda's mattress.

"That'll show you!" Without a backwards glance, Charlotte left the room. Had she stayed a little longer, she would have seen the cereal bowl she'd left there disappear.

At breakfast, Charlotte and Eileen had their usual two bites of toast and three swallows of milk, leaving all their leftovers on the table.

Soon, their father was in full we're-going-to-be-late panic mode.

"Shoes, shoes!" he cried. "Get your shoes on. Grab your backpacks. Let's go!"

Eileen dashed back to her bedroom. "I need something for

Sharing," she said.

"I've gotta get my lunch box," said Charlotte, running for the kitchen.

"Ahhh!" screamed their father.

When at last they were ready, he rushed them out the door.

No one thought to look back at the breakfast table. If Charlotte and Eileen had done so, they would have noticed that their dishes were now nowhere in sight.

Chapter 3

At the start of Eileen's class, the students sat in a circle with their teacher and had Sharing or "Show and Tell." Today it was Eileen's turn.

"Last week," she told the class, "my family went to an art fair and my mom bought me—"

She stuck her hand in her backpack, feeling around for the candle she had brought. Her fingers closed around something that felt like the right shape. "—this," she said, pulling it out and spilling the milk inside it all over the carpet.

The students goggled at her for a

few seconds then all started talking at once.

"A glass of milk?"

"Your mom bought you a glass of milk?!"

"It doesn't look like it's from an art fair."

"I think it's sour."

13

"Eileen!" exclaimed her teacher.

"That's not what I was going to share, Ms. Tonild!" cried Eileen. "I don't know how—"

"You shouldn't bring drinks to school without lids," Ms. Tonild scolded. "And certainly not milk unless you can keep it cold; it will make you sick."

"But, I didn't—"

"Never mind. Just clean up the mess."

Meanwhile, Charlotte's class was working on math problems. Charlotte stopped working to talk to her friend Rachel about all the things she had managed to blow up in her computer game.

"Charlotte! Rachel!" The teacher's voice broke through their discussion. "Have you finished your work?"

"Yes, Ms. Yancey," the two said together.

"Rachel, let me see it," Ms. Yancey demanded.

Rachel, who had finished her math, was told to amuse herself with a math game until recess.

"Charlotte," said Ms. Yancey, turning to her. "How much have you got done?"

Charlotte gulped. Slowly, she opened her math book to show her teacher her half-finished worksheet.

"Oh, Charlotte!" Ms. Yancey

gasped in horror.

Puzzled by her reaction, Charlotte looked down at her math book.

Lying on the open pages was the plate of slightly-eaten toast that she had left on the table that morning. Pieces of crust had come off the plate and there were crumbs all over the table.

"Charlotte," Ms. Yancey found her voice, "you know you're not allowed to eat at your work space. Look what a mess you've made! Did you even get any work done?"

Charlotte was still staring at the plate. "I don't believe it," she whispered.

"What?" said Ms. Yancey.

"I don't believe it. I don't believe it!"

"Charlotte, keep your voice down!"

"This isn't fair, this isn't right," Charlotte babbled. "She can't be doing this, how could she be doing this, she's not even here, is she?!"

"Charlotte, what are you talking about?"

"Glenda!" screamed Charlotte,

standing on her chair and looking all around the room.

"Glenda? Your sister?" said Ms. Yancey, uncertainly. "Do you want to see her?"

"No!" screeched Charlotte. "I want to kill her!"

Chapter 4

Recess finally came. Eileen was eager to find Charlotte to tell her about the milk she had found in her backpack and the toast she had found in her hat. She found Charlotte kicking rocks across the basketball court and looking rather upset about something.

Timidly, Eileen walked up to her big sister. "Charlotte?" she said. "What's wrong?"

"Everything," Charlotte grumbled.

"Did someone put milk in your backpack too?" asked Eileen.

"Milk?" Charlotte laughed. "Don't be ridiculous! No one put milk in my backpack."

Eileen looked disappointed.

"Someone put toast in my math book," Charlotte explained.

"Really? Me too!" said Eileen, looking happier.

"What?" cried Charlotte.

"I mean in my hat," said Eileen. "I threw the plate in the garbage but…" she pulled off her hat and showed Charlotte the inside, "…I couldn't get the crumbs out."

Charlotte glared down at the crumbs.

Eileen pulled back her hat nervously.

Charlotte looked her little sister in the face. "Eileen," she said gravely, "I think Glenda cursed our dishes."

"Cursed our dishes?" Eileen sounded awed. "That's why they've been following us around?"

"Yes," said Charlotte.

"You think Glenda's a witch or something?"

"I don't know."

"But she can fix it, right? We can ask her to—"

"Are you crazy? We can't ask her for anything. She might turn us into squirrels!"

"We have to do something!"

"Don't worry," said Charlotte. "Glenda's going to New York after school and she'll be gone all weekend. We can look through her stuff and find out how to break the spell on our own."

"Why is she going to New York?" asked Eileen.

"Oh, you know, she's singing at some Carnegie Hall place with her choir," said Charlotte, impatiently. "Did you hear what I said about breaking the spell?"

"So…we can stop dishes from following us around after school?" said Eileen.

"That's right," said Charlotte. "Just don't say anything until Glenda's gone."

With this understanding, the

two soon left each other. They did their best to get through the day as if everything were as it should be.

This was easier for Eileen who found no more dirty dishes. Charlotte, on the other hand, pulled a glass of milk from her coat pocket right after recess and found her bowl of soggy cereal (without a soggy fragment missing) in her lunch box.

Chapter 5

At home that afternoon, Charlotte and Eileen poked their heads around the hallway corner. Their father was standing by the front door with Glenda, going over her packing list.

Eileen watched Glenda with wide, worried eyes.

Charlotte was nervous too, but determined not to show it. "Any minute now," she said to Eileen.

"She sees us!" Eileen shrieked.

"Just act normal," hissed Charlotte.

Glenda waved. "Bye."

"Bye!" they said, waving back.

"Have fun in New York," said Eileen. "Sing spell. I mean well!"

"Good-bye!" said Charlotte again.

Glenda stood watching them with a funny smile on her face, while her father finished with the luggage.

Finally, they were gone. Charlotte and Eileen knew their mother was downstairs in her office, but they also knew she wouldn't come out unless there was a fire.

They rushed at Glenda's bedroom doorknob. Once inside, Eileen closed the door behind them, while Charlotte went to the bed and pulled back the covers.

"What are you doing?" asked Eileen.

"Eileen," said Charlotte, "these dishes have it in for us."

"You mean they're gonna kill us?"

"I mean," Charlotte continued, "that they won't follow anyone else. This morning I put that cereal bowl right here in Glenda's bed, and look!"

Eileen looked closely at the unstained mattress.

"It doesn't look like it was even

there," said Charlotte. "Whatever we do with these dishes, they come after *us*. No matter where we put them, they always come back."

"But I threw that plate I found in my hat in the garbage," said Eileen. "It can't come back!"

"Can so!" Charlotte insisted. "I told you I found that cereal bowl in my lunch today!"

A spooky silence followed.

Eileen was looking so worried now that Charlotte became uncomfortable.

"Hey," she said, more gently. "It's gonna be okay. We are gonna figure this out, break the spell and beat Glenda back. Right?"

Eileen nodded bravely. "Right," she said.

"Okay," said Charlotte. "Let's have a look around."

They searched Glenda's closet, drawers and dresser.

"No cauldron," Eileen reported. "No wand. No broomstick."

"We need to find her spell book," said Charlotte. She was running her finger along the rows of books on Glenda's bookshelf.

Eileen watched while Charlotte climbed a step ladder to reach the top shelf.

"They look like novels," said Charlotte. "But here." She passed a book down to Eileen. "Let's look

through them just to make sure."

They flipped through pages, hoping to find something suspicious. They thought that Glenda had a lot of books until they opened the cupboard under the bookshelf.

"Wow," said Eileen in amazement. "Do you think Glenda's read all these?"

Charlotte made a face. Normal people had lots of books. Glenda had lots and lots and lots of books.

They were still looking through them when their father came home from the airport.

"Charlotte? Eileen?" he called. "Where are you guys?"

"We're in—" Eileen began.

"Shhh," said Charlotte. "Let's get out of here."

Charlotte opened the door halfway and escaped the bedroom, dragging her sister behind her.

Chapter 6

Charlotte and Eileen had spaghetti for supper.

Eileen ate hers out of a bowl full of ketchup.

Charlotte made her own special sauce out of butter, honey, pepper and cheese.

When they had each eaten about half of their spaghetti, they jumped up from the table.

"Wait a minute," their father called from the kitchen.

"Why?" said Charlotte. "There's nothing left to do here."

The second the words were out

of her mouth, Charlotte's plate of spaghetti disappeared.

Eileen gasped. "Oh, where did it go? Charlotte, it's gone into your bed or something. You made it angry!"

"I didn't mean to," said Charlotte.

"Oh, please." Eileen got

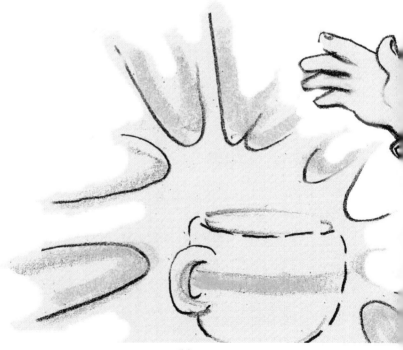

down on her hands and knees before
her own leftover supper. "Don't get
mad at me.
I'm done

eating, see, so I can't do anything else with you now."

Her bowl of spaghetti disappeared before her eyes.

"Nooo!" moaned Eileen. "Come back! Come back!"

Charlotte pulled her to her feet. "Silly, it can't hear you."

"What's all this noise?" said their father, coming back into the room. He looked down at the empty tablecloth. "Good. You've cleared the table. Guess who's coming upstairs early tonight?"

The basement door opened.

Charlotte and Eileen whirled around. "Mommy!" they said together.

The family spent a happy

evening playing "spit in the ocean" (one of the family's favourite card games) and "rat-a-tat-cat" (another card game).

Charlotte howled when she lost and screamed when she won.

Eileen giggled while their father covered his ears and made faces.

After a few rounds their mother returned to the basement. She came back up with a tray full of fruit, chips, peanuts, cookies and candy.

They grabbed handfuls of snacks while they played cards.

Charlotte never saw her mother fill the tray up again. But somehow the snacks kept coming. Every time she took the last cookie from the tray, she would look back to find another pile ready for eating.

"You know," said Eileen, sleepily, as she and Charlotte brushed their teeth that night, "maybe we should ask Mommy about Glenda."

"Eileen!" said Charlotte, sharply. "I told you we had to keep this quiet. If Glenda finds out—"

"But Mommy might be able to help," said Eileen. "I think she might know something about witches, you know?"

Eileen yawned and staggered off to bed, leaving Charlotte to wonder about the snacks that they had enjoyed earlier. It was a strange thing, she thought, that all those cookies hadn't given her a stomach ache.

Chapter 7

Charlotte's dirty dishes haunted her dreams that night. She was running down a dark tunnel and close behind her plates, cups, bowls and crumbs made threatening noises. She couldn't see just how close they were in the dark, but she was sure that any second now they would catch up to her.

She awoke with a start and looked wildly around. Her nightie smelled like sour milk. She saw an empty cup sticking out of her sleeve. Disgusted, she crawled out of bed and stuck her foot in the cereal bowl that was lying on the floor.

"No, no, nonononononono, noooo! This cannot be happening to me!" she wailed.

Dancing about in anger, she next stuck her elbow in a plate of spaghetti (leftover from supper) and sent it flying.

Losing her head completely, Charlotte ran from the room and bumped into—

"Mommy!" gasped Charlotte.

"Charlotte," her mother said, standing in the hall in her dressing gown. "What *is* the matter?"

In her agony, Charlotte forgot about keeping secrets. Before she knew what she was doing the whole story came tumbling from her mouth:

"Glenda got mad and cursed our dishes so they follow us everywhere me and Eileen they hunt us down and find us no matter where we are no matter what we do and Glenda's an evil witch and we can't find her spell books and the dishes won't ever leave us alone ever again, Mommy!"

There was a long silence.

"Oh," said her mother. "Well… why don't we get you cleaned up and then we can…talk about this."

Ten minutes later, Charlotte was in clean clothes and her mother had made them each a cup of hot chocolate. It was only 5:00 a.m. and no one else was up yet.

"So," said her mother, once they had sat down at the table. "Glenda put a spell on you?"

"Yes," said Charlotte.

"Why?"

Charlotte thought. "Because she got grumpy about doing the dishes," she said, remembering. "And she wanted me to help her do them when it wasn't my job and I was busy blowing things up on the computer. I tried to explain it to her, but she wouldn't understand."

Smiling slightly, her mother said, "There may have been something that Glenda was trying to make you understand as well."

"What's that?" asked Charlotte.

"It seems to me," her mother
went on, "that the answer is probably
in Glenda's spell book."

"But we looked *everywhere*," exclaimed Charlotte. "We couldn't find any spell books."

"You may not have looked *everywhere*," said her mother. "After all, witches don't need to use books made of paper anymore. We live in a more advanced society now."

"But—"

"Well…where do you keep your hobbies?"

പ്രവ്യ

"Eileen! Eileen, wake up!" Charlotte shook her sister awake.

"What?" Eileen opened her eyes. "Charlotte?"

"Get up! Get dressed! Hurry!"

"But, Charlotte—"

"Eileen," said Charlotte, "I know

where we can find Glenda's spell book!"

Eileen blinked and pulled a plate of leftover toast from under her pillow, scattering the crusts and crumbs everywhere. "Good," she said. "This spell is starting to bug me."

Chapter 8

Eileen found her leftover spaghetti in the bathroom sink and her glass of sour milk in her sock drawer. Charlotte decided that the only other dish likely to bother them anytime soon would be her plate of toast (the only item that had not yet appeared that morning).

With this hopeful thought in mind, Charlotte led a search on Glenda's computer.

"Are you sure you know what you're doing?" asked Eileen, as Charlotte double-clicked on files.

"Of course I do," Charlotte

assured her.

"I didn't know that your blowing-things-up game made you so smart," said Eileen.

"Well, it does," said Charlotte. "See!"

The file she had just opened was headed: *Domestic Witchcraft for Teens*.

"What does 'domestic' mean?" Eileen wanted to know.

"It's just code for 'evil'," said Charlotte.

"Oh," said Eileen. Then, looking at the screen, she said, "It looks like the whole thing is in code."

"What?" Charlotte scrolled down with the mouse. "No. Those are just the spells."

"Where are the unspells?" asked Eileen.

"What we need," said Charlotte, "is something in English to explain how—"

"There!" yelped Eileen, pointing at the screen.

A colourful picture filled the screen; it showed children being chased by dirty dishes. Beneath it were the words: "Schiebe die Schuld wo sie gehört."

Scrolling down a little further, Charlotte found more understandable words and read them aloud to Eileen:

"This is a level three vengeance spell used to punish the lazy and annoying. It causes people who do not clean up after themselves to face natural consequences in a magical way. Cast this spell on any one object and that object will follow the person responsible for it. This spell is usually used on dirty dishes (see picture) but also works with laundry, toys or anything else that you want out of your hair and into someone else's! The spell will last until it is broken which can only be done by its victims. Be warned: this means that you yourself cannot break the spell once you have cast it. Never fear! Even the most stubborn of children cannot put up with this spell for long and will soon give in to the idea of cleaning up after themselves in order to be rid of it."

At that very moment a mug of hot chocolate appeared in Charlotte's lap and splashed cooling hot chocolate all over her (not a drop landed on Glenda's desk).

"Oh!" said Eileen. "When did you have hot chocolate?"

Charlotte wasn't listening. She only gazed at the mug on her lap. Her

eyes lit up. "I've got it!" she cried. "I've got it!"

"What?" demanded Eileen.

"I know how to break the spell!" yelled Charlotte, running from the room and being careful not to spill what was left of her hot chocolate.

"But how could you?" said Eileen, following her to the kitchen. "It didn't even tell us how—"

"Yes, it did," said Charlotte.

She leaned over the kitchen sink, poured the hot chocolate down the drain and placed the empty mug with other dishes waiting to be washed.

Eileen stared. "That broke the spell?"

"For the hot chocolate it did," said Charlotte. "But we still have to show all the other dishes that we can 'clean up after ourselves' because Glenda cursed them separately. The *spell* only works on one object at a time, so the *unspell* has gotta work the same way."

Gleefully, Charlotte picked up a plate of toast that had just appeared at her feet and scraped every crumb into the garbage can. "Ha! I've just unspelled two of my dishes. I'm such a genius! I beat Glenda back. Hurry up and unspell yours, Eileen. I bet you anything I can finish first."

"Yeah?" Eileen challenged. "You have more than me."

With that, they both dashed about the house looking everywhere for their dishes. They were not in the places they had been in that morning, but they had not gone far. Eileen found her milk in her bookcase, her toast in her laundry basket and her spaghetti in her doll house. Charlotte found her cereal in her closet, her spaghetti under her bed and her milk in her art kit.

Five minutes later they had both "unspelled" their dishes. (They finished at the same time and could never agree on who had won the race).

"So," said Eileen, thoughtfully, "All this time that was all we had to do? Scrape out our leftovers? That's all it takes to break the spell?"

"That's what the book said," said

Charlotte. "But I guess we should wait to make sure it worked."

"But…" said Eileen, "if that's all that we needed to do, we could've done it in the first place and then none of this would've happened, right?"

"I suppose," said Charlotte.

"So," said Eileen, "if we scrape out our leftovers all the time from now on, this won't ever happen again!"

"We could try that," said Charlotte, doubtfully. "But I don't know…I think Glenda will always be evil just the same."

Chapter 9

After a full day without dirty dishes chasing after them, Charlotte and Eileen knew that the spell was gone for good. That night they slept soundly in their cosy beds and dreamed of clean clothes and comfortable lives. When they awoke the next morning they enjoyed both more than they had ever enjoyed them before.

Eileen soon forgot any fear or anger she might have felt toward Glenda. Charlotte was not afraid or angry anymore either. But she was bursting with pride to have been the one who undid a witch's evil spell.

"Oh yeah. Uh huh. Uh-huh, uh-huh, uh-huh!" she said as she danced her victory dance. "Who da man? I da man! I am just the most amazing—"

"And I helped," said Eileen.

"And you helped," Charlotte agreed. "But *I'm* the one who figured it out."

Charlotte was still feeling very pleased with herself the night that Glenda came home from New York.

"Guess what?" she said boldly to Glenda. "Guess what I did while you were in that Carnage Hall?"

"Carnegie Hall," her mother corrected. "It's a famous place."

Charlotte rolled her eyes. "Not if *my* sister was in it."

"Was Carn-a-gee Hall big?" Eileen asked Glenda. "Even bigger than Van-yay?"

Vanier was a performing hall

inside one of the local high schools.

"A lot bigger," answered Glenda. "Also a lot older. And with a lot more ghosts."

Eileen shivered. "You saw ghosts?"

"Yeah right," said Charlotte, sensing one of Glenda's ridiculous stories coming on.

"I heard them," said Glenda. "Ghost voices from people who sang so high that their notes got stuck in the ceiling. When they left the hall they left their singing voices behind. And now that's the only place you can hear them."

"Did that happen to you?" breathed Eileen.

"No," said Glenda, smiling. "I sang the low notes with the altos."

"What about your boat tour?" asked her father. "Did you get a good look at the Statue of Liberty?"

The talk of New York went on and on. So Charlotte had little chance to brag to Glenda about beating her spell.

Glenda soon saw for herself that the number of clean dishes in the kitchen had grown. She smiled quietly to herself. From the look on her face, it seemed that Glenda did not think that *she* was the one who had been beaten.

Chapter 10

That weekend, Charlotte's friend Rachel slept over. Saturday morning, she, Charlotte and Eileen had waffles for breakfast.

As soon as she was done eating, Rachel got on the computer.

Charlotte scraped her leftover waffles into the garbage can and then pulled up a chair beside her friend.

Eileen washed and dried her plate for good measure. She went into her parents' room to play dress-up.

Their father left to buy groceries. Their mother went down to her den to write.

It was an uneventful morning until Glenda decided to get a head start on the day's dishes.

She got through the cups, forks and knives without complaint. And then…

"Rachel!" she called. "You didn't finish your waffle. Come and scrape out the leftovers."

"I can't," Rachel yelled back. "My mom will be here any minute

and if I don't blow up twenty things in the next ten seconds, I'll die!"

"Yes," Glenda agreed. "But when your mom gets here you'll go home and then you'll never —"

"Shut up!" snapped Rachel. "I'm trying to…oh man! I died! You

distracted me!"

"Are you sure you won't scrape out your leftover waffles?" asked Glenda, dangerously.

"Rachel, maybe you should—" Charlotte began.

"I'm sure!" said Rachel, turning

around to glare at Glenda. "I don't have time for waffle plates, it's not my job to wash the dishes and you ruined my...what are you muttering ab—?"

Rachel's jaw dropped in mid-word; the plate in Glenda's hand had just disappeared into thin air.

Glenda returned to the dishes before Rachel could find her voice.

"Wh-where did that p-plate go?" she asked Charlotte.

Smiling weakly at her friend, Charlotte said: "You might want to check your bed when you get home."

Made in the USA
Charleston, SC
04 May 2014